The Pulse Remains

Graveside Reads Vol 1, Issue 1

Rob Grimoire

Undertaker Books

THE PULSE REMAINS

1

- -

ANY MEASURE OF LIFE as it lies at our feet is difficult, especially after the war. Blood still stains the marshes and the hands of every person here, and in different ways.

My father's blood marks every structure, laying bricks for buildings that his family could not enter. My mother's hands and body made food that her children weren't allowed to eat—her love and care were ripped away from us and placed in the house, her flesh and soul consumed by those who owned her. Bits of their spirit are still in bondage to this place.

My husband was a proud man born without shackles, knowing that all freedom is not equal. James Turner. An intelligent, loving man ready to take on this system for true liberation. A soldier for the north, known for his bravery and his ability to heal wounds, knowledge passed down from mother to son. They were of the Haudenosaunee people of his land. He always said that his cleanliness was unrivaled on the battlefield, where soldiers he cared for would lose fewer limbs, and fresh water was always on the fire. James made sure that when Jacob was born, we had a pot boiling.

He returned with something missing from him, coming back a dissolute, broken man ready to run north, looking desperately to give up the farm and go. James drowned himself in drink to dull the pain of his wounds, those that long healed and those that never had a chance to. He found his solution to it all at the bottom of a bottle. A drunken vision of liquor departing its vessel, ultimately mirrored by his death, and the burning of his lifeless body wrapped in burlap.

I would like to believe he had a choice, that he didn't have to drown his sorrows in alcohol, but living here in the truth of it all I understand him, my banjo being the bottom of my bottle, and it's endless. The only time I played while away from my people was at his burning, where we met a few of the white soldiers he served with. As the flames whipped, my voice vibrated with the rhythm of the fire, sending his soul to rest, washed over in the river to Orun.

As his body burned, my eyes wept for his soul with a furrowed brow, angry that he left us that way. We miss him, all his warmth, love and strength. We miss him.

Before the embers died out, my shoulders felt a chill, and my jaw clenched as if winter blew through. It was the batting of wings—the eyes of vultures were ready to pick our bones clean now that James was gone.

We've been working the farm for a year since my husband's passing. Jacob is fourteen now, getting tall, looking more like his father every day, and starting to sound like him as well. Quickly running out of money after James' death, and needing a loan from the bank, we had to switch our crops to cotton, which we never wanted to grow. Knowing this plant drew blood from black hands, shattered families apart, and pushed people past breaking and into death—all for the clothes and sheets that the brown bodies in the house had to wash and fold—we still had to go back to it, and pledge a year's worth of crop to the bank, to get the loan.

Charles Smith, the bank owner, expressed interest in buying our farm, circling it as soon as my husband died. He can hide all he wants under that potato sack mask when they ride at night, but my ear recognizes his voice anywhere, his tone is one of weakness hidden. He was overjoyed to lend us the money, grinning, offering us luck from one mouth, while plotting our demise with the other. My prayers flow to Oya, that she hears his wicked wishes the way my ear tunes to them...

Mother Oya, she who has never been lost to us, transcends time and space, navigates our broken, murdered language, and finds a place in our forced one. Mother of Storms, Keeper of the Container of Fire, Watcher of the Gate between life and death, the undefeated warrior demanding justice. It's a comfort just to speak her name. And a fright to witness her power, as she rains down life for our crops, or destroys a town in a torrent.

On this night, Smith takes the farm down the road, the Reeves farm. We hear the screams of our neighbors and see the torches in the distance, like fireflies in the night, moving away into the woods. We hear the Reeveses beg for mercy and scream their lord's prayer. Jacob grabs his father's gun propped up near the front door, his hands shaking while he loads the weapon.

"Son, put down the gun and make sure the back door is secure."

"Yes ma'am," he says with a heavy brow. At least if he is in the back and I need him to escape, he can, and quickly, barricading the door behind him with the wooden bar. His father built safeguards in our home, and we have kept them up.

Oh, Oya-Iyansan-an, hear me. I'm asking you in all your might that their poor souls are taken to the gate and welcomed by your nature. Mother of Nine, accept more children into your river and have your song lead a torrent to those who wish us harm.

As soon as I speak Oya's name, a thundering shakes the whole house like a stampede of wild beasts, striking at my heart. Cracks in the floorboards radiate heat and shades of red light come bursting through the damaged boards. As the planks tremble, the scent of seawater permeates the air around me. The floor grows soaking wet as water bubbles up, and there is a pull on my warm, wet feet, traveling up my legs and back, making them heavy, shaking my foundation.

The weight of the unknown presses me to the ground, my head under the water that's crept into my home, applying pressure across my whole body. I struggle for air, trying to kick and swim to the shallow surface. My back is released, and it drags me through the water and across the floorboards, splashing as it pulls me out of the flood, and pins me against the wall next to where my husband's sugarcane machete hangs, oozing with blood. Its copper blade cries out for more, its handle rattling with rage felt deep within. My eyes shut, pulled tightly together by fear. As tight as the knot in my throat, the ethereal pressure covers my body, fixing me to the wall, soaking wet and unable to move. Her voice is known to me at that moment for the first time, angry, yet comforting and warm, like a fever in my ears.

Pick up the sword, child. Dance with the storm and fire, sing them to sleep, death to life, life to death.

My arms become engulfed in white fire, and my body acts on its own, frantically trying to put the flames out, silently, my speech lost to me. I feel no pain, but there is a want in my body and an emptiness in my soul. Silence follows, and the absent sound of death is in tow. Opening my eyes, I see an impossibly dry floor, my unbelievably dry body, dust in the air made visible by the beams of moonlight shining through the frame gaps of the front door.

Jacob runs from the back to me. "What happened, Ma?"

"I just tripped, Son, I'm ok."

Can't explain to him what just happened without looking like I have a sickness. My plan is for him to leave this place without me, and soon. If he's worried about me, this will be harder for him. My conversation with death will be a long one—there are vultures waiting, and the woods will be forced to welcome my blood in its roots like they welcomed my parents, and their parents before them.

We venture out the next day, early always, because to be caught in town as the sun starts to rest is dangerous. Walking through the woods, we see the remnants of rope on different trees. The forest witnessed these crimes, unable to shield itself as countless bodies swung, the leaves begging for an end to it all and the roots covered in blood, echoing the desperate cries of the strange fruit the woods are forced to bear. We eventually walk up to the awfulness of the Reeves family, husband and wife both hung and nearly decapitated. Their eyes bulge from the pressure of the rope, blood still attempting to soak into the black soil, pooled and congealed. Their pale faces forever twisted in pain telling me their final story.

And evil stands behind us.

"Why, good morning, Samantha." An eerily cheerful voice springs out of the woods. It's Charles, admiring his work, I'm sure.

"Good morning, Mr. Smith," I respond, head down, gritting my teeth because we both know the truth of the matter before us.

"Good morning, Jacob."

My son looks up and nods.

"Poor folks. I wonder what happened here? Who would be so hateful as to do this to a preacher? He just sold his farm and the church to me as well. What a shame. My advice, as a banker, would be to sell that small patch of land you have to me, and head up north where they want you people. I'd hate for anything like this to happen to y'all."

His threats are real, and my fingertips lose heat as he's making himself known with the stench of murder on his breath, hidden from others by his southern drawl. He nods, and then trails off, heading in the town's direction.

As soon as he's out of sight, Jacob gets his knife so we can cut the Reeves family down. Reverend Reeves's brother, Steve, lives on the other side of town and sells fruit to us. We can inform him so that he can collect their bodies and give them a proper burial.

Their corpses contort as they hit the ground like a second death.

Oya, accept them please.

Kneeling and closing my eyes in prayer, a hand settles on my shoulder, so I grab it. It's cold and clammy. "I'm scared as well, Jacob."

"Ma, let's go," Jacob says from afar.

My eyes flash open to see the dead woman's hand on my shoulder, her eyes, milky blue and glazed over, with a fly crawling around on one of them. Her head moves up from its slumped position, slowly. She opens her mouth agape with a little blood flowing out. She grunts and says, "Eeparrei!"

My arm moves in fright, pushing the hand off me, and I scuttle backward as the body drops to the soil, screaming silently and filling the space with my physical fright. The rapid beating in my chest drops into my stomach, and I swallow the morning mist, gasping for air and trying not to scream.

Not knowing how far Charles is, and not wanting him to come back, both hands cover my mouth, not letting one peep escape as my back drops to the ground with no support.

Jacob sees my panic and runs back, leaving the cart near the Lee River trail. He picks me up and I dust myself off. The woman's corpse is still by the trunk of the tree where we left it. Maybe I am sick. These things can't exist outside of a sick person's world, things seen in the fever. Either way, Jacob needs to get out of here. That cold wind is blowing, and the caws above us are getting louder every second of every day, and falling fast like the sun is setting on my life, MY LIFE, not his. Keep going as if this didn't happen.

"Jacob, we need to get in and out of town before sundown," I say to him, trying not to break my mask. Just a boy and he's seen so much already.

We travel the road to town, taking the trail around back, where we do business at the back door, folks not wanting to be seen with us, but willing to take our money. There is no place for us on Main Street, but there is plenty of space for us under. We need more leather strapping, strings for my guitar, and goods from farms on the other side of town. As Jacob is off, I'm getting things with the last of our savings—things for him to take with him.

"Ma, we need to sell the farm and leave," Jacob says. "As soon as the rest of these blue coats leave the area, it's going to get worse. Even they look at us with contempt, Ma. We can read and write. People have been killed for less."

"I'm not leaving!" I say, clenching my fist. "I know how much Smith is offering, but if you think, Son, do you truly believe he will let us leave town with it? When have you heard back from anyone? Why is it every time he buys someone out there are new pyres ablaze, their light flickering up to touch the sky, struggling to reach home, and a smell all too familiar? If we sell, we die. If we don't, we die, but you WILL leave this place, Jacob."

"What do you mean, Ma?" he says, with a confused look on his face.

"As soon as I sell this place, I'm going to stay here, with a candle lit in the window, moving about inside while you take the Union boat upriver. They will take me, but you will have a chance."

"No!" he exclaims, hyperventilating and shaking like a leaf. "I won't leave you."

"You have no choice, Jacob. This is—well, was, our hope for you and it's only my hope now. To survive beyond this place of suffering. I don't want your spirit to haunt this land, and your father wouldn't either. Go down and pick up my strings; we will finish this later. We have other things to do," I said, cutting off the argument.

He looks at me with his father's eyes, says "Yes ma'am," and sprints four doors down, his feet carrying him fast, his heart wanting to fight for us both to leave.

A rumbling breaks my concentration, shaking everything around me. Then the sound of women screaming "The Union Army!!"

Several soldiers ride up. One I instantly recognize as Bart Calvert, a man my husband served with who introduced himself at James's burning. He sees me, turns, and says something to his men, and as they all spread out, he rides over to us. The dust that covers his horse and blazer blows behind him, his silver hair moving with the breeze, his horse tired and breathing heavily like the journey was a long one. The sharp-jawed man stops his horse just shy of us. He spits to the side as his horse drops her head in the water trough for a drink.

"Mrs. Thorne, it's good to see you again. You changed your hair! How is Jacob doing? Is he around by chance?" he says, urgency in his voice.

"Jacob is down the road getting my strings."

"I'm sorry to hear that, I wanted to offer him a job tending our horses. His father was the best healer in the field. He saved my life, and countless others were able to return home because of him. How is that farm he talked about so much?"

"It's good, but we're about to sell."

"To Charles Smith?" he asked.

"Yes."

Jacob yells, "MA!" Rushing back, as Bart moves closer to me.

"Good afternoon, Mr. Calvert," Jacob says, sticking his hand out to greet the soldier, getting in between Bart and me.

"Good afternoon, Jacob." Bart shakes Jacob's hand, and his hand tightens as the muscles in his forearm tense up. Jacob focuses all his strength on the grip, locking eyes with Bart, attempting to draw a line in the sand with his power, I think. Several people look on with disgust, not at them shaking hands, but at the Blue Lincoln soldier who would just as easily burn everything down without a second thought, changing their way of life forever, back here again, reminding them of what they lost in the fire of war.

"We're here to investigate land theft and murder that's been reported by a local, unnamed source, and all seem to be centered around Charles Smith," Bart says.

"We need to leave this place Bart, I have a feeling that Charles, no, I KNOW Charles will be coming for us next. I will testify to his crimes," I say to him, ready to put my life up sooner rather than later.

"You will become a target if you stay here, Samantha, and not just of Charles Smith. Making a statement to us officially will put a target on your back and it will be made public," he declares.

"NO," Jacob says, and I can see the idea flow, entering him as he speaks. "That's how we leave Ma. We can sell to Charles while Mr. Calvert is here, and leave under Union protection, together. After we are safe, you can testify."

Bart smiles. "James always said you were a clever young man, and he was right. My men will check the bodies and Reeves's farm, and after you make that sale, we will escort you to the boat to start your way up to Pennsylvania. You have three days, then we leave." As he rides away, we head off to the other side of town to collect the rest of our wares.

"Do you trust Bart Calvert, Ma?" Jacob asks.

"I don't have a choice. I'm betting on your father's work with him," I say.

My mind should be at some ease knowing that we will have help leaving, but I can feel a change in my hands. A stiffing. A message from the sky that soon there will be rain, and lots of it.

Word spreads quickly across town about the Reeveses' deaths, and some heads hang low, emotions high and unspoken for the loss of their warmth.

The Reeves family, one of the only white families that were good to us, always treated us with respect and dignity. It wasn't a surprise when we discovered that they were helping escaped ones get further to freedom. A red door railroad stop on the way to the North Star. It was discovered after the war ended, and Pastor Karl Reeves was more comfortable sharing his experience, thinking not about his family's safety, but about the occupation of the city and what it provided to him. Comfortable enough even to state how he'd fooled Charles Smith on multiple occasions, hiding his slaves who had escaped at the church, and getting them one more step closer to freedom.

We knew that we were little more than property and less than rodents to the Confederates, but we never thought Smith would be brazen enough to murder a white family for their farm and for revenge, feeling the hole that the efforts of Karl Reeves left in Smith's pockets through Reeves's large, red church door.

As we come up on the Steven Reeves farm, we recognize Charles Smith's white horse tied to a post. "We should come back tomorrow, Ma," Jacob says. "The rain will start soon, and we won't be able to get this far,"

"No, Jacob, we will hold back here and wait for him to leave. We need to get these fruits. I can make preserves tonight for our trip." I hope the tone in my voice and the smile on my face reassure him and calm him down, so we wait a bit and watch.

Charles walks out, passes money to Steve Reeves, and shakes Steve's hand. "It wasn't hard for you to get them out of their house, Steve, but Karl would trust his brother, right?"

Steve looks off, the shame on his face barely hidden.

Charles unties his horse, and gallops down the road, leaving a thick dust trail in his wake.

As soon as we fail to hear Charles's horse striking the earth with its hooves, we continue down the road and wave down Steve before he goes inside.

"What do y'all want to buy?" he says, with a toothless grin on his face, hiding the wad of cash in his shirt.

"Well, we have something to tell you," I say with a heavy head.

"Let me guess, my brother is dead." He cuts me off, right at the knees. "Yeah, I know. I just sold my share of the family land to Smith," he says, with sadness for his brother and sister-in-law on his face. "Come with me, girl, I have some extra apple baskets in the barn, and I'll give you a deal; I need to get rid of them. Watch the horse, boy, and ya mammy can come to grab them," he says.

I'm usually with Mrs. Reeves when we come into town to visit Steve's farm, and he's never given me pause. He is the only one who has these fruits in town, and we need them to make those preserves. Who knows when we'll be able to pick up more food after we make the trip out of here? Every time we've come here, we haven't had any problems, but after seeing Steve with Charles, I feel a sense of uneasiness.

As we walk to the back of the barn a flash of light from the apples, reflecting the sun's rays, catches my eye from the back corner of the barn. As I walk in to get them, Steve's footsteps trail behind me, the puffs of dust from the dirt floor become larger as he gets closer to me. Getting to the apples before he can, my hands grip the bushel and, in a panic, I swing around, drop my basket, and the apples spill, rolling everywhere. Before I can start to pick them up, he continues closing in on me.

He puts his arms up to embrace me, pressing me against the barn wall. He won't stop, entering a space where he is not welcome. I look down, and everything around me becomes present. I can hear him saying things, but the words are unclear. My hands twitch, unsure of their next move. I start to look back and forth on either side of him for a way out and my voice loses itself. I can't cry out for Jacob, that would be the death of him.

There is no escape, no way out of this situation. His breath is hot and stinks of shit and liquor.

He's coming closer to my face. My skin starts to heat up like I have a fever in my chest, and it travels to all corners of my body, from my fingertips to my toes. The heat continues to rise, and my breath is faster, my chest beating so loud it feels like it's echoing in the barn.

He squeezes my shoulders tighter, pinning my arms to my side, but removes his hands immediately, steps back and turns his head. "You're sick with fever, girl! Go on, get your apples, and get out of here!" I drop down, grab the crate and the bruised and broken apples quickly, and run as fast as my feet can carry me to the door,

My voice crackles, showing itself again as I call out to Jacob. "Let's go, now!" My rusty brown hands have a reddish hue, matching the color of my hair, and my arms are wafting steam like water in a boiling pot.

"Ma, are you alright? You've been acting a little off since you fell last night. Did you hit your head?" Jacob grabs the basket from me, and feels my arm, seeing the steam rising from it. "Mama, your arm..."

In my haste, I cut him off. "But I feel just fi..."

The words never complete their journey from my mouth to his ear as my body melts, as I lose control of my legs and sight. He's panicking, screaming for help while I drift down and down, into a river of black. Sounds muffle, and I faintly hear him begging like no one is coming.

My body feels light, lifted, settled in, floating on down a waterless river.

The swaying back and forth wakes me. At a steady pace, I can hear the squeaking of that old wheel on our cart, uncertain who's moving it, hoping my Jacob is okay and he's pulling us home.

I hear whoever is driving the cart muttering quietly, "You are gonna be alright, Ma. You are gonna be okay." So I'm certain it's Jacob. He sounds just like his father. In my stupor, I can see the twilight before the darkness blankets us, the last rays of light banded across my face and body.

I hope we are close to home.

The smell of the freshly lacquered posts on our porch slithers like snakes in water, strong pine vapors stabbing at my nose and pushing my eyes to tears.

"You're gonna be okay, Ma." Jacob comes close to help me get into the house. He holds my legs and gently helps my feet to the ground, then comes around to support me as I attempt to stand with him.

There is a tunnel of consciousness of things around me, but my mind is clouded in dense fog, and my legs are walking through thick mud that's just not physically present. My mind, swirling about, and a voice within reach, one that is unyielding in its search for me.

Steady.

We enter the house, and Jacob helps me to my bed.

2

- -

"I CAN MOVE AGAIN!" I yell in great joy. It's dark in here... "Jacob, where are you, Jacob?"

I realize I am lying on a hard surface, and I put my hands down to brace myself and get up slowly when I feel the grit and walls of a wooden box, its grains reading my death in the darkness.

Bang! Bang! Bang!

"JACOB! GET ME OUT! HELP!" The scent of fresh earth consumes me. "I'm NOT DEAD! Why bury me? Why?"

Help yourself, child.

"Who are you?"

You KNOW who I am! she says as the box rumbles.

"How do I help myself? HOW?" The fever returns, warmth pulsing through my hands and feet. A light from below me appears and I can see the roots growing into this coffin. The brightness increases, and I realize that it's me, that my legs are on fire and it's moving up my body. I kick and scream as the flames engulf me slowly, but I feel no pain, only a desire to get out. To be free, a fight in my heart that beats in the hearts of all things, and like the grass in a strong wind, I submit to it. I stop fighting and let it take me.

The box is completely covered in a cleansing alabaster blaze as I watch my corpse set aflame but not burn. What a strange feeling, to see myself die.

Yet I remain.

The image gets smaller until it's nothing more than a glint. The body does not weigh the absence of light, more tiny candles surround me in the dark, floating in all directions and so small I can only see the white fire on their dancing wicks.

I am your mother, young elder of the night, and you are my hands.

I never knew my birth mother, but I know her story. I know her words and her mother's words. The words were spoken mouth to ear and never out loud so that we would never lose you to the slaver's religion, or have your warmth beaten out of us.

Yes, I've never felt the pain of silence, and I heard your call to me, Aje, so I spirited you here just outside of Orun, the place where the sun sets on life, and to me, the sword's edge eternal, guarding its gate.

I feel eyes on the back of my neck, and the heat of a fire at my heels. My body turns as I will it, and behind me, she sits on the back of a large beast. The beast is massive, with curled black horns, alive with the crackling fulminations of the storm's light, eyes glowing red with forward intention, smoke billowing from its nostrils, and hooves covered in thick fog.

The woman's eyes shine like metal in comparison to her dark, black skin, absorbing all light and life. Her hair of bundled red vines whips in the wind with black ends lashing. Red, furrowed, intense eyebrows shape her pupil-less golden eyes, excited and ready for battle with an inquisitive half-smile showing teeth of pearl. Her body is adorned with a blood-red chest plate, shaped to expose the left side of her chest, bracers, and a long, colorful flowing skirt, water like and crashing with waves as its seafoam frills dance along the hem.

"Oya!" I say, my voice breaking like glass. "Mother...am I dead?"

No, she answers. **You spoke to me through the void and the waters deep, and I want to show you the power in your blood. You fight against what you don't know. Your hands stiffen and your voice contracts to nothing and you refuse to draw power from your ancestors. The more you fight, the more your body warns you not to. Allow your voice to be as free as the wind, and spurn storms with your words, fire with your fingers. Consume my power. Consume it, but don't let it consume you.**

The beast digs its hoof into the ground and kicks up the fog, pawing clouds and thunder into space. The smoke from his nose starts to fill the black, swirling in a torrent, making it harder to see. I feel Orun's presence slipping away from me as I wake to the rooster crowing and Jacob blotting my face with a wet cloth soaked in fresh water. I must have been out all night.

"Ma, you—you're awake!" he says quietly with a smile and tears in his eyes. "How are you feeling?"

"I'm feeling okay, baby." I hold his hand with confidence and gratitude. "You carried me all the way home and we got here before dark yesterday. Jacob, your father would be proud of you."

"It wasn't too hard, Ma, but that wasn't yesterday, it was the day before. You were asleep all day," he says.

"What! But the Veseys' gathering, I...I had to play for them!"

"It's ok Ma, I already covered for you. Ms. Vesey even came down to help me with you and she cooked for us."

"That was kind of her to do, and thank you, Jacob. I'm gonna freshen up and head down to thank them."

Grabbing my banjo and case to head out, the cracking open of the front door hits me with day's light, taking me back. Something I've missed dearly, I let it bathe my skin while kicking rocks in the road on my way to the Veseys' house with a tin of biscuits to thank them and to apologize for not being able to play for them yesterday.

Making my way down the dirt road, I notice there's a lot of commotion in the house's direction. People conversing and laughing, kicking up a little dust moving from the front to the back of the house through the wire-gated entrance of the small garden.

"We sold it!" Beck Vesey pops out of her chair sitting on the side of the road as soon as she sees me.

"That's why your things are outside?" I respond, puzzled at the sight.

"Charles made us an offer on our property, paid us in gold, and we're crossing over to the Lowcountry today before sundown to stay with family."

"But Beck, you know what Smith is capable of; why risk it?"

"I'm not worried about that buckra. He doesn't know about the path we take to get to the island through the basement dock of the church they burned down. Y'all should come with us, Sam. You and Jacob can stay with us and our family until you see fit," she says, carefree in her confidence.

"Let's hope not. He purchased the new church the Reeveses built after the war," I tell her.

"He told us during the sale, he paid Steven money for his brother's half of the land as well," she said.

"Thank you, Beck, but we have other plans. Let me play for you and your family on this wonderful day." Their faces light up with joy while I strum my heart away, and their bodies move double time, hauling items to their carriages. The weight of things seems to melt away for them as I play, picking up the pace in tandem with me picking at my strings. My fingers fly across the fretless sea of mahogany, thickening the air with messages of hope and moving on from this life to the next.

I can see my bright new home, over the horizon,
Life from flesh, years into bone, over the horizon.
Moving from one place to another, over the horizon
I won't misstep, and I won't stutter, over the horizon.
The North Star, watches me, over the horizon.
Before the sun's gone, I will be, over the horizon.
I am home.
I am home.
I am home.

Almost unnaturally, they finish within the hour.

"You sure you won't take us up on that offer, Sam?" Beck says.

"Thank you, Ms. Vesey, for helping Jacob take care of me. Fare thee well, and be blessed on your travels," I say politely, once again declining her offer and heading off home.

They finish setting up to cast off on a small vessel that barely fits the rest of their belongings and overflows with hope. As they set off, my body follows down the road, waving goodbye across the marsh.

"See you on the other side, sister!" Beck shouts, as the boat heads downriver toward the islands, and toward their new beginning.

Flailing my arms about in joy, my hope sets in, my mind begins to wander into a daze, dreaming about the day we will be sailing off and hoping that our plan works. My hands start to cramp again and shake uncontrollably. Everything starts to slow down, and my eyes become unfocused, darting everywhere. My thoughts leave me, and the sound of the water crashing against the land floods my ears. Then the trance is broken abruptly, and a man screams, "FIRE!"

A loud *boom* shocks me. My knees buckle, dropping me down to the ground, snapping me out of my haze. The whistling of the iron ball brings memories of war, and my eyes connect to the boat.

Beck's face loses its smile, contorted by the impending atrocity. Our eyes meet and she stretches out her arms to reach mine, as I reach for hers. It feels like an eternity; her face marked with a fear I understand.

The blast pushes me back into the bushes, taking with it my ability to breathe, and shrouding my senses. A long, loud ringing in my ears and a blinding flash disorients me, and the disturbed bank waters rush up my dress to my knees from the edge.

"See you on the other side, sister!"

Confused and taking in my surroundings, the rhythm and cadence of the time and space around me move me to a familiar place in all its smells, sounds, shades, and light. There is only the family casting off to the island and Beck waving happily. My ears then tune in sharply to heavy metal being wheeled toward the bank in the thicket of trees across from me, the wooden wheels weeping under the pressure of the mass of metal. The bushes give me cover from what is about to come to pass. The plants are familiar to me now; their fragrant yellow flowers smelling of honey will be corrupted by gunpowder soon. The iron ball rolls into the tube with a clink to the bottom of the barrel. My body stands and my mouth opens to warn them without any thoughts of my self-preservation.

"FIRE!" A voice, vaguely familiar, but hard to pin down in the chaos the first time around. The pitch I'm certain I know, but the anger is foreign, distorting the voice.

The cannon explodes with killing intent. My voice carries out like the roar of a beast, "GO HOME!" Before the ball can meet its target, a bolt of lightning rips through the air without a cloud in sight, bright and indigo, striking the ball down. A rush of air pushes the Veseys' sails out of range, thick fog rolls into the water's edge and blankets the area as thunder follows close behind the purple bolt, shaking the trees. In the cover of white, my frame vanishes, running home as fast as possible.

Everywhere my limbs move, the fog follows, wrapping its cool mist around my body as if it were flowing from my heart and commanded by my soul to move with intention, cloaking me from all, and all from me. Almost blindly and moving lightly, I shift through the ditches and across dirt roads—my only guide the fence that separates our land—feeling the change of the posts the closer I get to home. The fog stops and a tiny breeze clears the air around my home, making it visible in patches to me, and Jacob is standing outside looking for me like he knows something has happened.

"Ma, did you hear that loud bang? I was worried, so worried. I cannot wait to leave here," he says.

"Go inside, we need to pack." Tomorrow is the day, and the storm is getting closer; I can feel it in my bones and see its warnings in the sky.

My mind keeps looming and looping, weaving the day's events into something I can try to understand. That man's voice. I know that voice.

Outside, a horse neighs, and someone knocks on the door. It's Bart. The door opens and he takes off his hat, a gesture strange to see from a white man interacting with us.

"I came by to let you know that while we can't arrest Charles yet because the witness wouldn't come forward to testify to the crimes seen, I want to help finish the sale of your property by delivering the contract for you to sign. I've talked to Smith, and he only wants what's fair when it comes to paying for your home and land. He also wants you to come play before you leave, as he said he's heard so much about your skills with the banjo. I will be in attendance along with my best men, so you need not worry about the old bastard. I'll witness the signing, and deliver you both to the docks shortly after, given this rain lets up. If not, you all can camp down with us until it passes. The rest of my regiment and my commanding officer should be heading into town tomorrow."

"I don't want to play for that man, but I will get this over and done," I respond, as my hands begin to stiffen up and my body urges me to leave it all and just go now. And at this moment, I understand James and his spirit of escape very well.

"Continue packing and we can get you out of here. I owe James that much, and much more." He grabs my hand and tips his hat, smiling from ear to ear. The level of respect he has, bordering on admiration, scares me, but I trust that James is watching us and that his last gift of friendship to Bart Calvert will get us to safety.

As he takes his leave, the rain picks up. I peek out of the window to see him ride off toward the Smith plantation. Several bolts of lightning pop in the dark in the time it takes an eye to blink, lighting up the area like a flash of sun. Dust that would be spiraling about is now constricted by a brief heavy downpour that converts it all into mud, making the planned trip to the Smith plantation a messy one.

I can't help but think of James at this moment, especially looking at my son packing our things. James would be proud of Jacob, growing up and learning more about the limited world we live in, expanding his mind with books outside of the marsh.

As soon as we open the door to head out, the rain subsides. Jacob, nervous as expected, asks if we should take the rifle just in case. "No, Son, Bart will be there, and we won't be long."

"But I don't trust them, Ma, I don't trust any of them. Bart...he looks at you like Pa used to, it makes me feel weird. I don't like it," he says.

I never noticed how he *looked* at me because out of survival, I never look at white folks in their faces, especially the men.

Maybe it's admiration and gratitude for James saving his life, and if it is, Jacob would understand that.

"Your father saved his life in the war, healing his wounds and sending him home to his family again. He's just grateful for him. I wish more of them were grateful for him."

"I can only hope you're right," he says.

"I pray Oya wills it and blesses our journey." My voice squeezes out as my throat tightens saying those words. My chest constricts, and a heavy worry weighs itself across my heart.

3

MOVING DOWN THE ROAD, the thick, reddish-brown mud makes the trip feel like an eternity, as the horse struggles to wade through it.

Light sprinkles of rain started to drop as we left the house, and we picked up speed so we wouldn't get soaked. In my chest, I feel the heavier storm approaching, and I can hear Oya in its impending wind. My hands are starting to loosen up, and my heart slows. Everything seems like a strange waking dream, one out of my control.

We arrive at the end of the road and the beginning of the Smith plantation, lit by poles with bells of fire dancing in the lanterns in line with the alley of oak trees.

We are greeted by Bart at the end of the cobblestone walkway, and he has his men take us and our horse to the back where the service area is. Inside the house, we walk down a dimly lit hallway past the kitchen. Briefly, I lock eyes with a beautiful little girl no older than fourteen with white ribbons in her hair, cooking for the guests. Her vision looks glossed over when our eyes meet, a sight I've seen before.

It isn't the look of someone who gets to go home after work.

Her eyes cry out for help and when she sees me, her hand reaches up to her mouth quickly to cover, like she was stopping herself from asking for help for the sake of us both.

The poorly lit room where they had us wait and warm up feels heavy and uneasy. Furniture is arranged in no order, covered in white sheeting, with two chairs and a table by the door for us, and a single candle.

Above the flickering fireplace is a picture of the Smith family, covered in splatters of dark paint. Jacob moves closer to the painting. "Ma, what happened in here? It looks like pigs' blood on the wall, and the fireplace is all burned up."

"Let's get ready, son, pay no mind to that, let's get ready." I say to him, holding my hands to my chest to warm them, and to say a small prayer. Something happened here, quick and brutal.

I set my case down on a table and open it to consult with my banjo and take a moment to adjust my thoughts in this haunted place, the walls screaming, its ghosts trapped, dying without knowing freedom.

As I reach for my banjo, it meets my hand in the middle, as if it jumped into my arms, ready for me to inspect it and play. The tension of the drum is perfect, and my strings are warm and ready to play, but tuning is always needed.

"Miss, they will be ready for you shortly," says one of Bart's men. "Your son can follow me to the living quarters; there is a seat by the service area where he can wait outside until you are done."

The look of defiance on Jacob's face at the thought of leaving me alone is prevalent.

"You will be able to hear me, so go," I say with a smile.

He gets up slowly and follows the large man down the dark hall near the screen door.

"They are here and I'm ready if you are," I hear Bart's voice say while I'm tuning, but not from outside of the room, from inside. It's coming from the marbled, water buffalo hide drum of my instrument.

"They are the last witnesses, and the rest of the Union officials cannot interview them, Bart!" Smith says.

"Yeah, couldn't catch the message before it went out, but my commander will be here tomorrow, and they will be gone by then. We'll put their bodies in the back at their home and set fire to it all," says Calvert.

Fire... *Fire!* The stark realization of my situation strikes me, my hands begin to sweat, and I now know. It was Bart who tried to kill Beck and her family, but I think I always knew, that pitch and tone.

"You still owe me for the Vesey property, Bart. You allowed them to get away." Charles scolded Bart like he was a child who'd spilled his milk.

"It was bad weather, not my fault at all. We have been covering for you anyway, so as far as I'm concerned, we're square," Bart said.

"You must get her and her son away from my home, and then the next four miles are clear. The Turners' house is in the middle of that lot. Let's hurry and get the signatures here to make it all clear on the paperwork. Hell, the Veseys escaping will do nothing but help us look more legitimate, as your commanding officer can interview them about our deal. We've worked too hard and gone too damn far for this girl to wreck it all. After I got rid of the traitor Reeves, I should have shot them both dead right there in the woods, but I know you want her for a spell, and I'm a man of my word." Charles chuckles, and Bart follows suit.

"Yeah, I have a predilection, and she's gonna scratch my itch before she dies," Bart says.

They laugh harder, vibrating the drum and my strings.

Jacob was right about them, and Oya has been here this whole time, warning me in the air and the trees. She spoke to me through the dead and dream, and allowed me to draw from her power in times of need, even if I wasn't aware of it. They won't kill us here, this I know, so I must listen to the rain for our chance to escape. I'll play for them and draw more power from her, until their blood drops like the heavy rain. I must keep Jacob safe; I must.

I understand it now Oya, that the only way out is through.

Bart knocks twice and enters the room, his face covered mostly in an angled shadow, the light available painted across his eyes, making them visible. The first time I've ever truly seen them: one green, and one gray.

"We're ready for you, Sam. Remember, one song, and we can get you out of here."

"Sure thing, Bart," I respond, knowing his true nature now. Walking out, I turn and look at Jacob down the dark hallway. I can see him. He can't see me, but he stands up anyway as his vision cuts right through the darkness.

"Ma, are you okay?" he asks.

"We will be." My words expose me in their tone, flat and slightly trembling.

"Go out back and get your horse ready, boy. We will be done here soon," commands Bart.

Jacob walks out back to where the soldiers are, smoking near the stables.

Walking into the room, the intent of these men is palpable, making light of our lives and our deaths, and comfortable with it. Singing with suppressed rage is different. My eyes dart across the room at the many weapons on the wall, out of reach, and two guards by the door making me feel closed in. The way Bart stares at Smith with disgust is genuine, making me understand that the way he looks at me with want is also real.

I play while they drink and celebrate. When I feel my fingers start to go numb, I stop with a discorded strum and ask for the contract so we can make our way down the road. "Just calm down girl, we will give it all to you soon," Bart says, as the men laugh.

He's finally letting his mask slip, because that is the first time he's not used my name while addressing me. Charles stands and puts the page and pen on the table in front of me. "Sign and I'll have the men bring your horses around.

After I sign the contract, he throws the bag of gold at my chest, knocking the wind from me. "Here ya are, Sam, hope to see you again soon," Smith says. "Good doing business with ya. Oh, send my regards to your husband." I close my eyes, clench my jaw, and breathe in deep. James' face flashes in the dark, his smile graces me, and his courage sits next to mine, I must stay the course. "Oh dear, please excuse me, I'm very drunk, and it's been a long night. My apologies," Charles says with a grin.

"Enough of that, Charles," Bart says, smiling. "Let's leave, Sam."

I glare back at Charles Smith and look him in his soulless, arid blue eyes as I walk out. As soon as I get outside, I need to position us to cut into the forest and run the hidden trail Reeves used to help slaves escape.

The storm sees me, tingling throughout my hair, making it stand on end, my braid breaking the ribbon and unraveling as it puffs out to reach the moon. At the first break of heavy rain, we'll run. Bart escorts us out down the long walkway, just him and his horse, as his men stay back. I don't understand why it's only him, but this will make our escape easier.

As we walk the mare, I look over and whisper to Jacob, "As soon as the thunder strikes, turn the horse and dart directly into the woods, fast."

Jacob nods his head yes without hesitation. I get onto the back of Bart's horse, and we start down the muddy road. I smell the rain in the air, the stress of moisture that will finally be relieved as the clouds release their weight.

About a mile down the road, we track. A large bolt of lightning punches through the gray sky close to where we live. As the thunder hits our shoulders, my arms rear back and I push Bart off the horse, then Jacob and I fly into the woods.

We don't get far. A gunshot scares the horses, who buck up, leaving us on the muddy black forest floor. It's Charles Smith with Bart's men; rifles pointed at us.

The moon provides shattered light, showing its power among the clouds in a struggle to be present, shifting in brightness and shade. Bart's men grab Jacob and drag him through the mud by his ankles.

Even though I'm screaming, I hear Bart behind me. "You'll pay for that!" I yell. He raises the butt of his pistol and swings it. Nothingness consumes me.

The drops are heavy and make more visible the brutality of each strike as water reacts to violence in the rain. The storm light illuminates the stage for their theater of hatred as they beat the boy. His mother wakes and with no waste of words, continues fighting with her life to save him, powerless and forced to watch them slowly murder him. The rain moves erratically, slowing down and stopping, then restarting as she shouts out at them, attempting to break away from that man with two faces.

I watch too, as she screams her soul out to join with his. "We trusted you Bart, we trusted you! Why...WHY?!" Her heart breaks as the one with pale eyes shoots her in the chest. Two last breaths, taken in unison to beyond the flesh. The men head back to their shelter after my bolt strikes a tree and sets it ablaze near them, leaving the bodies.

This was hard to witness, but my warnings were clear. The boy had no fear and wanted only for the safety of his mother, but his mother wanted to continue, to seek them out and make them suffer.

My call moves in the wind and void, beckoning, and she draws in the sum of it, breathing in life with a strength unseen before. As the rain continues to grow in strength, so does Sam, her dress absorbs the darkness of the mud, the blackness of her pain. She moves one knee up, pushing her hand deep into the black topsoil, stumbles to stand unsuccessfully, and strikes out against the earth itself. Her voice breaks the sky, splitting the thick cloud above her in two, breath bleeding fire, lighting the area with steam flowing all around her flaming voice.

Born again, she crawls in the water and sludge to her son and cradles his head on her lap, weeping heavily, rocking and singing his lullaby in her heart as if it's stuck in her throat. She feels the pain of his final time on this plane, and the resolve of his blindingly bright spirit as it moves into the next.

She sees the eyes of his villains in this grove, surrounded by black willows where they took her ancestors and in taking Jacob's life, the possibilities of tomorrow. The black belt, where blood stains the soil dark.

"I was a fool to believe this would work."

The rain watches as she takes his cooling body and places it in the red flames of her house, where nature struck her home and set it ablaze. As he is reduced to dust, she reaches out for her banjo, which cuts through the air, whistling to her hand from another place, to sing for him—

He rises in my heart,

alive in just a day,

as I hold him to my breast,

my troubles fade away,

but my worry's here to stay.

My worry's here to stay.

She sings until the rain turns the roaring fire into only orange embers and ash. Lightning flashes, brushing the top of the trees with a glow, exposing her through the dark and bathing her in white light for a short time.

She tosses her banjo aside, walks toward the smoldering pile, slowly digs her hands into the grey, glowing mash, and scoops a handful of it up like water, and as soon as she touches it, her hair, now a large puff, begins to render itself as red as copper. Her brown skin glimmers in the night, untouched by the rain.

As she presses the ashes of her heart onto her face and neck she opens her eyes, now obsidian black, and looks sharply up into the sky, and with a deep breath in, pulls the air down into her being, bending the trees toward her from the power, as if they are bowing to recognize her status.

I lose all sense of my godly self as I see through Oya and I, Sam drawing power beyond my comprehension. She lifts her arms and raises our body, branching out and extending herself past the veil to Orun.

I and I, flow into her and she into me, a god bound to her until we are done, and I move with the wind past the dark clouds into the space between, searching for those who took my heart, so that I can return the favor.From two, to one.

The tapestry of our mind is open, documenting the story of our ending, and beginning. We fully succumb to the fury and spirit, accepting fate as the storm, and draw power from it. Lightning streaks across the sky like the many tails of a flywhip, lashing out, eager to touch the ground.

From two, to one.

Seeing them all as the moon sees, never leaving, refusing to be hidden by daylight. My heart beats with a death rattle, not giving one ounce of compassion to the current of life again.

The only way to the end is through, and I will tear. I will tear it all down until it's clean.

I will start it all over.

It's cold up here past the dark, churning clouds, chilled right through to my hollow bones as I move through the thin, liquid sky.

Parting the water in the air, I see the plantation and the soldiers hunkering down, trying to get their ranks and bosses to higher ground. Landing near the long road leading to the estate, I've never seen the grass this strong and beautiful, whipping with the storm, taking it like it's a zephyr, forgetting for a second that I see and think through another form now.

They panic and rush, calling out to their God and losing their voices to mine and the rage of my storm. My body changes slowly, fluid translucency comes to solid focus, returning from air to flesh, and in time my full form emerges, takes flight as the torrential rain subsides, floating along the muddy path, staring at the sky where the clouds break clear just for me.

The eye of the storm beams down on the men. The peace of my firmament blows calmly as moonlight begins to blanket their collective prayers gathered in hearts and mouths, happy that they survived the storm.

Invocations to their god are shattered by the rising heat, and cutting right through the lingering mist is I, death incarnate, with open arms engulfed in white flames mimicking the moonlight. I come with a deathly embrace. The soldiers' weapons don't work against me, so they drop everything, try to run.

I am now witnessing. A harbinger tasked to scorch the earth. The soldiers start to scream, their clothing soaked, still reacting to the intense heat from my body that boils the water in their blue jackets, steam rising and burning their flesh, cooking them alive.

Eyeing Charles Smith and Bart running into the home, I rise and push forward. Touching the shadows, I cast myself within the silver clouds and move within them easily, casting them away with my light. This strange sorcery in my blood is familiar to me, allowing me to bridge to the place of my son's death while my voice rings in the trees across their blood-soaked roots.

My husband sends his regards.

Floating up to the front of the plantation, my fingers and toes tingle and sparks flow across my body into the ground. My heart beats no more, replaced with the churning of this storm that started on the coast where my foremothers were taken, following the path of bones and hantés to this coast, building power as it traversed the path of suffering to reach me.

The doors are nothing, no locks, chains, or man can hold me back as I move through the house. They have made their way out the back, not knowing they will never get away.

Before I continue my pursuit, I shed more light on the room I sat in before my death. The sheets move with the flick of my finger, and I see the blood-stained furniture, barely dried blood all over the walls, and a pile of children's dolls like the ones I had when I was a little girl. In the fireplace are the smallest bones, and two long white ribbons. Empty bottles of alcohol and shattered glass cover the floor.

Pulling their pain into me, the little girl speaks in my ear from the void "Help me, please. I'm trapped here."

I will, child, I will. My breath blows the roof off the house, shattering it into splinters, and those spirits caged by this place escape.

The wind sings as it takes buildings and homes, collapsing Steve Reeves's entire farm, twisting violently, and crushing him in the process.

Charles and Bart get to their horses and race toward the boats that are completely drowned by the waters I rose, now at the bottom of the bank.

I make sure they hear me coming with one last song for them.

All praise her and witness her tide of blood. Your houses will flood.

Taken into the black mud.

All praise her, she lights a spirit lantern.

The rapture will burn. Then rising fires take their turn.

They hear this as they run. Then, they are stopped by the river that's flooded far inland toward the wooded tree line. They can go no farther.

I feel the souls of my ancestors, the blood calling out for me to avenge them.

"Sam, that's you, isn't it?" Bart voice cracks as he slowly pulls his saber from its sheath. The hilt rattles as he shakes in fear at the sight of changed, dead woman floating towards him.

"What are you doing Bart? Kill it!" a panicked Charles screams, pushing Bart toward me.

"Let's j-just calm d-down," Bart says.

Did you enjoy yourself, Bart? I know what you have been wanting. I know what you did.

Dropping his sword, he pulls his revolver and exhausts the ammo. They both watch the rounds pass through my incorporeal body and into the trunk of a willow behind me. The rounds dig themselves out of the tree, dropping to the ground. The tree's roots speak my name, and I kneel on one knee. They get louder, until my hands drive deep into the black soil where my fingers seek their intentions.

The pull of haunted, buried metal just below the surface is shown to me. Bullets and broken swords of the slaveholders' war vibrate up my arms into my shoulders and chest as my conversation with the dead is fruitful. The sloshing, bubbling, and popping of the weapons drawing themselves from the soil is the language spoken here. They suspend themselves in midair, frozen and waiting for a god's command.

Fire!

They fly toward Bart, metal glinting and gleaming in the moonlight like jewels running him through, burying it all in his flesh and tearing him from limb to limb, and this time, without the mercy of my husband's care. My arms move to and fro and the metal follows, conducting his death in a symphony of pain. Charles watches in horror as Bart is torn apart, warm blood splattering all over his suit and face. What is left of Bart lies in the mud breathing erratically and my shadow travels up to him slowly.

You took something from me, and I'll take something from you now.

Taking his saber, with a swift and sure hand, I sever his head from his body. I grab it by the hair and lift it from the mud. His face continues to twitch, mouth moving, still begging for life. His eyes roll around while I dangle Bart's head, still dripping with blood, in front of Charles. I throw it at Charles, right at his face, breaking his nose and knocking him out.

When my shriek wakes him, he's in the sky with me, floating above the storm's eye. With his voice lost to fear, his eyes scream a terror I've seen in the eyes of the broken and downtrodden, black-skinned people of the sun, and by his hand.

All those children.

'I'm just destroying my property,' you said to your wife as you murdered them, is that right Charles Smith? All those children... I say while holding the little girl's ribbons.

He sees his plantation on fire from up high and can feel the heat of the flames. The once-trapped spirits circle it, dancing around the fire, waiting for Charles to come home.

He can't speak because he doesn't deserve to. I've sealed his mouth shut, but his mumbles beg for life, and today he will understand hopelessness, right before he is sent to his hell.

Slowly, we commune through the void again, and the disembodied ones lower Charles into the flames, his muffled screams making them circle faster around the flaming house. They drop him on the floor in that room, and a broken wall covered in fire collapses on him, igniting him as he struggles to get out. The spirits stop and push the rest of the walls down on him, then they scatter across the sky like shooting stars.

The storm continues to destroy everything in its path, leveling houses and pulling trees from their roots. Flood waters raise the tired, beaten bones of the long forgotten so they can witness the destruction of the fields they slaved in and the plantations that shackled them, to watch Oya burn it down and wash it all away.

As I reach out to Orun, my body is engulfed in white flame. I'm pulled into the vastness of the infinite sky. Turning back, my ascendence is rapid, and the picture of my life becomes water clear. The land grows smaller the higher I go. The whites, blues, and greens of the orb from high above eventually turn into a blue speck of sand.

Oya speaks to me. **It's time to give your heart to the stars, child. Your vengeance painted your essence in ash and blotted gray across the sky, seeding clouds and exorcising the land, and now your core will brighten the North Star where you will burn brightly still. As your tears fill the drinking gourd, your fire will burn infinitely, guiding those who still need its light. While your body fades, the pulse remains.**

Acknowledgements

To my family and extended family. Whitney, Renji and Remy, I love you all and appreciate your support and dedication listening to me mutter on about ideas I have, lol. My heart lies with y'all. To my mentor Paige L. Christie, a phenomenal author who encouraged me to "Use all the words" love you, Paige. To Alex, I'm forever grateful for you encouraging actions and words, you push me to be better than my last sentence, all the time, every time and in every way. To my Multiverse family, the amount of love I receive from y'all is impossible to measure, and truly spans the multiverse. If you think I missed you, I didn't and never will, the list would be crazy if I kept going, lol. I love you all and I am forever grateful for the support and crazy love you have shown me.

Thank you.

About Rob Grimoire

Rob Gilmore (He/Him) (writing as Rob Grimoire) is a father, nurse, musician, a huge fan of comics and consumer of almost all things horror, science fiction and fantasy. He's a multi-genre author who started writing in November 2022 after a wonderful experience at Multiverse Con in Atlanta where he proudly serves at the A.D. He's woven tales published with Manawaker Flash Fiction Podcast "Regalia" in audio format, a novelette titled "The Pulse Remains", the horror story "Cordyceps Angelus" featured in the anthology Dark Spores, the 4th installment of "Stories We Tell After Midnight" from Crone Girls Press, an Afrofuturist short story "Quicksilver" featured in MVmedia's Funk anthology series "Spacefunk!" and a poem titled "Crash Out" in Mocha Memoirs Press' anthology "A Crack In The Code: Cybertonic Stories Of Rebellion.

https://linktr.ee/RGrimoire

If you are a fan of horror stories and tales,
you'll want to follow Undertaker Books.
We're bringing you stories to take to your grave.

www.ingramcontent.com/pod-product-compliance
Lightning Source LLC
Chambersburg PA
CBHW031000310726
48969CB00008B/2410